Curious George®

GOES SLEDDING

Adapted from the Curious George film series
edited by Margret Rey and Alan J. Shalleck

Houghton Mifflin Company Boston

Library of Congress Cataloging in Publication Data
Main entry under title:

Curious George goes sledding.

"Adapted from the Curious George film series."
Summary: George, the curious monkey, goes sled riding
and saves a child from disaster.
1. Children's stories, American. [1. Monkeys—Fiction.
2. Snow—Fiction] I. Rey, Margret. II. Shalleck,
Alan J. III. Curious George goes sledding (Motion
picture)
PZ7.C9215   1984   [E]   84-16827
ISBN 0-395-36637-2 (lib. bdg.)
ISBN 0-395-36631-3 (pbk.)

Printed in Japan

DNP   10   9   8   7   6   5   4   3   2

"It snowed last night, George," said the man with
the yellow hat. "Let's try our new sled."

George and the man with the yellow hat went
to the bottom of the hill.

"You can climb the hill, George," said the man,
"but don't get into trouble."

At the top of the hill, Mr. and Mrs. Ramirez were
watching their children playing in the snow.

Lisa and Paul were making a snowman.
Their little brother, Jimmy, was helping.

George wanted to make a snowman, too.

He started to roll a snowball.

The snowball got bigger and bigger until it was
so big that George couldn't see over it.

"Watch out, George," called Mr. Ramirez.
"You're getting close to the edge of the hill."

But George didn't pay attention.
Suddenly the snowball rolled over the edge.

It rolled down the hill, turning faster and faster—
gathering more snow as it went.

"Watch out," someone cried. "Here comes an avalanche."

The snowball knocked over some skiers. A boy
on a sled got covered with snow.

"That monkey up there did it!" shouted someone.
"Let's catch him."

George ran away as fast as he could.
He jumped over a snow fence and hid behind it.

Now he was safe. He peeked out and saw little Jimmy.

Jimmy was all alone, trying to climb on a sled.
The sled started to slide toward the edge of the hill.

"Watch out, Jimmy!" shouted his mother. "Get off that sled!"

Jimmy couldn't hear her.

But George knew what to do. He ran toward the sled

and jumped on it right behind Jimmy.

George held on to the boy and
steered the sled with his feet.

They were heading straight toward a tree stump.

But George steered the sled away from the stump.

Mr. and Mrs. Ramirez came running down the hill.
"Jimmy, are you all right?" cried Mrs. Ramirez.

Jimmy just laughed. It had been so much fun.

"There's that monkey who knocked me down,"
shouted a boy.

"Leave him alone. He saved my Jimmy," said Mrs. Ramirez.
"Three cheers for George!"

Just then, the man with the yellow hat rushed over.
"So there you are, George," said the man.
"Let's go for a ride on the sled."

And that's what they did.